READ-TOGETHER TREASURY

FAIRY TALES

publications international, ltd.

Cover illustrated by Richard Bernal
Table of contents illustrated by Ute Simon

Louis Weber, C.E.O.
Publications International, Ltd.
7373 North Cicero Avenue
Lincolnwood, Illinois 60712

3rd Floor, 3 Princes Street
London, W1R 7RA

www.pilbooks.com

8 7 6 5 4 3 2 1

ISBN 0-7853-7913-4

Publications International, Ltd.

A NOTE ABOUT THIS READ-TOGETHER TREASURY

This is a special book. It is designed and written to be shared between an experienced reader and a beginning reader, taking turns reading aloud.

The treasury is extra-wide so that it can be easily spread across two laps. The experienced reader—Mom or Dad, Grandma or Grandpa, even an older brother or sister—sits on the left and reads aloud the left-hand pages. These pages are written using the classic storybook prose that children love to hear, but may not yet be able to read on their own.

The beginning reader sits on the right and reads aloud the right-hand pages. These pages are written especially for early readers. The type is larger and less intimidating, the vocabulary is basic, and the sentences are short and simple.

This book provides the perfect opportunity for a young reader to hone his or her reading and comprehension skills. The positive experience of reading together with a loved one will encourage a love of reading in children. And the quality time spent as you take turns reading may be the greatest reward of all.

Please enjoy this unique book, full of stories to read aloud, stories to treasure…stories to share.

Child of the pure, unclouded brow
And dreaming eyes of wonder!
Though time be fleet and I and thou
Are half a life asunder,
Thy loving smile will surely hail
The love-gift of a fairy tale.

–Lewis Carroll
Through the Looking-Glass

TABLE OF CONTENTS

Jack and the Beanstalk

Adapted by Lisa Harkrader   *Illustrated by John Manders*

Once there was a woman who lived in a little cottage with her son, Jack. Jack and his mother were very poor. And very hungry. It hadn't rained in a long time, and their garden had shriveled into weeds. Even their old cow had stopped giving milk. One day Jack's mother told him to take the cow to market to sell. "Get as much money as you can," she said. So Jack and the cow set off toward town. On the way, they met a stranger.

"I see you're going to market," said the stranger. "You won't get much money for such a sorry-looking cow, but I'll trade five magic beans for her."

"Five beans?" asked Jack.

"Five **magic** beans," said the man.

So Jack gave the man his cow. The man gave Jack five beans. Jack ran home.

"Mother!" said Jack. "I sold our cow."

"For five beans?" asked his mother.

"Five **magic** beans," said Jack.

Jack's mother threw the beans out the window. But the next day, there were no beans. There was a giant beanstalk instead.

Jack scrambled onto the beanstalk and started to climb. He climbed up and up, all the way through the clouds. And there, at the top of the beanstalk, he saw an enormous castle. Tired and hungry after his long climb, Jack thought someone in the castle might give him something to eat. He set off along the path that led to the castle.

When he reached the castle, the huge door swung open. In the doorway stood the tallest woman Jack had ever seen. "What do you want?" asked the woman.

"I—I'm hungry," said Jack. "And thirsty. Would you give me a drink of water and something to eat?"

The woman frowned at him. "Well, you're not very big," she said. "I don't suppose you'll eat too much or drink too much or cause too much fuss. Come in and I'll see what I can find. But you'll have to eat quickly and then be on your way."

Jack followed the huge woman. They went into a huge kitchen. Jack climbed onto a huge chair.

The woman gave Jack a huge bowl of oatmeal. She also gave Jack a huge cup of tea. Jack began to eat.

Soon he heard a huge *thump, thump, thump*. Footsteps!

Then he heard a huge voice.

"Fee—fi—fo—fum. I smell the blood of an Eng—lish—man," said the voice.

"My husband!" cried the woman. "Quick! Hide! If he sees you, he will eat you for his dinner."

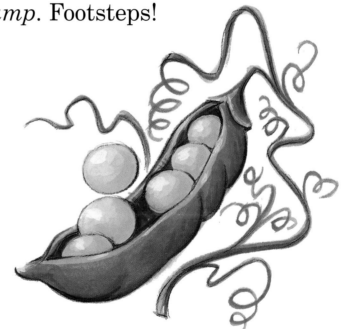

Jack scurried onto the huge table and hid under the huge teacup. He sat very still. *Thump, thump, thump, thump.* The giant's footsteps grew louder. Then they stopped. Jack heard the giant's huge voice.

"One, two, three, four, five," boomed the giant.

Jack lifted the teacup and peeked out. The giant was counting stacks upon stacks of gold coins. Jack stared at the gold. With that much money, he and his mother would never be poor or hungry again. Jack scrambled back under the teacup and waited.

Finally, the giant stopped counting. He had fallen fast asleep at the table. Jack crept out from under the teacup and tiptoed across the table. He grabbed a sack of gold and ran from the kitchen. He ran from the castle. He ran to the beanstalk and climbed down. He gave the sack of gold to his mother.

"Gold!" said Jack's mother. "Now we can buy food."

Jack and his mother bought food. They planted vegetables in their garden.

But it did not rain. The garden dried up. Soon the gold was gone.

"I will get more from the giant," said Jack.

He climbed back up the beanstalk. He went into the castle. But Jack did not see gold coins. He saw gold eggs.

The giant had a hen that could lay gold eggs!

"Lay!" boomed the giant. The hen laid a golden egg.

The giant smiled. Then he stopped. He sniffed the air.

"Fee—fi—fo—fum. I smell the blood of an Englishman!"

howled the giant. "And I'll find him this time."

The giant stomped around the castle, sniffing as he

went. But again, Jack was safely hidden away under a

teacup, and the giant did not find him. The giant returned to

the table, huffing and puffing from all that stomping around. In fact,

he was so worn out, he soon fell fast asleep.

Jack saw his chance. He ran across the table, grabbed the hen, darted from the

castle, and climbed down the beanstalk. He gave the hen to his mother and told her that the

hen could lay golden eggs. From then on, Jack and his mother always had enough money for food.

But the hen was sad. "The giant has a golden singing harp," she said. "If she ever stops singing, the

giant will melt her down and make gold coins." Now Jack was a good boy, and he did not want the hen to be

sad. So Jack climbed back up the beanstalk. He found the magic golden harp singing the giant to sleep.

"La, la, la!" sang the harp. The giant yawned.

"La, la, la!" sang the harp. The giant shut his eyes. He was almost asleep.

"La, la, la!" sang the harp. The giant snored.

Jack tiptoed to the harp. He reached out his hand. He grabbed the harp.

"La, la, la—HELP!" sang the harp.

"Shhhhh," said Jack.

But it was too late. The giant woke up. "Fee—fi—fo—fum. I smell the blood of an Eng—lish—man!" boomed the giant.

Jack picked up the harp and ran toward the door.

"You again!" yelled the giant. "You're the one who stole my gold and my hen. I won't let you steal my harp, too. I'll catch you and eat you for my dinner instead." The giant chased after Jack. Jack raced toward the beanstalk.

"LA, LA, LA!" screeched the harp. "Who are you and why are you stealing me?"

"I'm not stealing you," said Jack. "I'm saving you. I'm taking you away so the giant can't hurt you. My mother and I live in a little cottage. You and the hen will be safe there."

"I'll be with Hen?" sang the harp. "La, la, hurry!"

Jack held the harp tight. He ran down the path. The giant thundered close behind. Jack could see the beanstalk just ahead.

Jack got to the beanstalk. He climbed down as fast as he could. He could hear the giant behind him.

When Jack got to the bottom, he gave his mother the harp.

Then Jack grabbed an ax. He chopped down the beanstalk.

Boom!

The beanstalk crashed to the ground. So did the giant. And that was the end of the giant.

Jack, his mother, the hen, and the harp all lived happily ever after.

Rapunzel

Adapted by Kate Hannigan   Illustrated by Kathi Ember

Long ago and far away, there lived a husband and wife who longed to fill their house with children. One day the wife announced that they were going to have a baby. "I can't eat just bread at every meal now," she told her husband. "I'd love to taste the green rapunzel that grows in the garden next door."

The husband knew it was wrong to take the leafy lettuce, but he wanted his wife to be happy. He decided to sneak into the garden when no one was looking. Just as he clambered over the wall to take some of the rapunzel, he felt a cold rush of air.

"Ah-hah!" screeched a shrill voice.

It was a witch! The garden was hers!

The witch did not want people in her garden.

The husband was scared.

His eyes grew big.

His knees knocked.

He could not move an inch.

The man looked at the witch.

"I am sorry," he said. "I just wanted some lettuce for my wife. She is having a baby."

The witch was furious, but she had an idea. "Go ahead, take as much of the leafy lettuce as you want," she said, sneering and stroking her pointy chin. "But in exchange, you must give me the baby the moment it is born. I will raise it as my own child."

Too frightened to utter a word, the husband scooped up the lettuce and ran home as fast as he could.

Months passed, and the wife's appetite for rapunzel grew and grew. Each night, the husband would

sneak over the garden wall and take more. "Perhaps the witch has forgiven me," he hoped to himself.

Finally, one bright and sunny morning, the baby was born. It was a beautiful baby girl! "We shall call her Rapunzel, after my favorite food," said the wife.

Just then, the door burst open and the witch stepped in. "Rapunzel! What a perfect name," hissed the wicked witch. "Since you took the rapunzel from my garden, I will now take Rapunzel from you!" And as quick as that, she was gone with the baby.

The witch took
Rapunzel far away.
She locked Rapunzel
in a tower. She did
not want Rapunzel
to leave.

Rapunzel lived
there for years.
She never saw
anyone but the witch.

Rapunzel grew older. Her hair got longer … and longer … and longer.

The witch visited every day. She stood at the tower and called out,
"Rapunzel, Rapunzel, let down your golden hair."

When Rapunzel heard the witch's call, she would lean out of the window and unwind her long braids. The witch would climb up the braids as if they were ropes.

The witch knew it was wrong to keep Rapunzel locked up in the tall tower. But she was afraid that Rapunzel would run away, leaving her alone in the world. The witch never unlocked the tower door to use the stairs, and she didn't dare keep a ladder around in case anyone wanted to take Rapunzel away.

"What happens outside the tower?" Rapunzel asked the witch one day.

"Nothing good," replied the witch. "It's best if you stay right where you are."

"Are there other people to talk to out there?" asked Rapunzel.

"No one as kind and loving as I am," said the witch.

And the witch was indeed kind to Rapunzel. But there had to be other good people out there beyond the fields, thought Rapunzel. And there had to be a whole exciting world to see.

Rapunzel did not want to hurt the witch's feelings, but she was growing restless.

Rapunzel was bored. She had nothing to do.

She brushed her hair.

She counted the clouds.

She tapped her toes.

Her only friends were the birds.

Rapunzel made up songs in her head.
She taught the songs to the birds.

The birds loved to hear Rapunzel sing.

And they were not the only ones!

One day a prince rode by the tower. When he heard a sweetly singing bird, he stopped his horse and tilted his head to take in the lovely tune. He pulled out his spyglass and searched the trees, hoping to see the songbird. But instead of spying a bird, the prince spotted Rapunzel singing from the tower window!

Just then a dark figure approached the tower and called up to the mysterious maiden. "Rapunzel, Rapunzel, let down your golden hair," called the witch. The prince watched as Rapunzel dropped her braids and the witch climbed up into the tower. After the witch left, he saw Rapunzel crying at the window.

"I must rescue her from this prison," said the prince. He tried the door, but it was locked. So he called

out, "Rapunzel, Rapunzel, let down your golden hair!" Rapunzel peeked out of the window. "I'm here to rescue you," said the prince.

Curious, Rapunzel let down her braids. The prince climbed up into the tower.

Rapunzel and the prince talked and talked.

The prince told her about his home.
He told her about
the people who lived there,
the books he read,
the horses he rode.

Rapunzel liked the prince's stories.
She said, "I want to
see new people,
see new places,
read books,
and ride horses."

As they talked, Rapunzel and the prince fell in love.

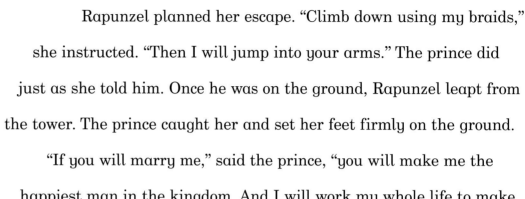

Rapunzel planned her escape. "Climb down using my braids," she instructed. "Then I will jump into your arms." The prince did just as she told him. Once he was on the ground, Rapunzel leapt from the tower. The prince caught her and set her feet firmly on the ground.

"If you will marry me," said the prince, "you will make me the happiest man in the kingdom. And I will work my whole life to make you the happiest woman." Rapunzel knew in her heart that he was good, so she agreed to marry the prince. They jumped onto his horse and galloped off toward his castle.

The prince was so excited, he invited the whole kingdom to meet Rapunzel and celebrate their happiness. Long lines stretched out the castle door as people from all corners of the kingdom came to meet the new princess.

An old couple stood in line patiently. "Did you hear her name?" whispered the old woman. "Could it be?"

Soon it was the old couple's turn. They stepped forward.

"Rapunzel," said the old man, "do you know who we are?"

Rapunzel looked into their eyes. "You are my parents!" she said. "We can be a family again!"

Rapunzel's parents lived in the castle with Rapunzel and the prince.

And they all ate the leafy lettuce called rapunzel with every meal.

King Midas

Adapted by Lisa Harkrader   *Illustrated by Kevin O'Malley*

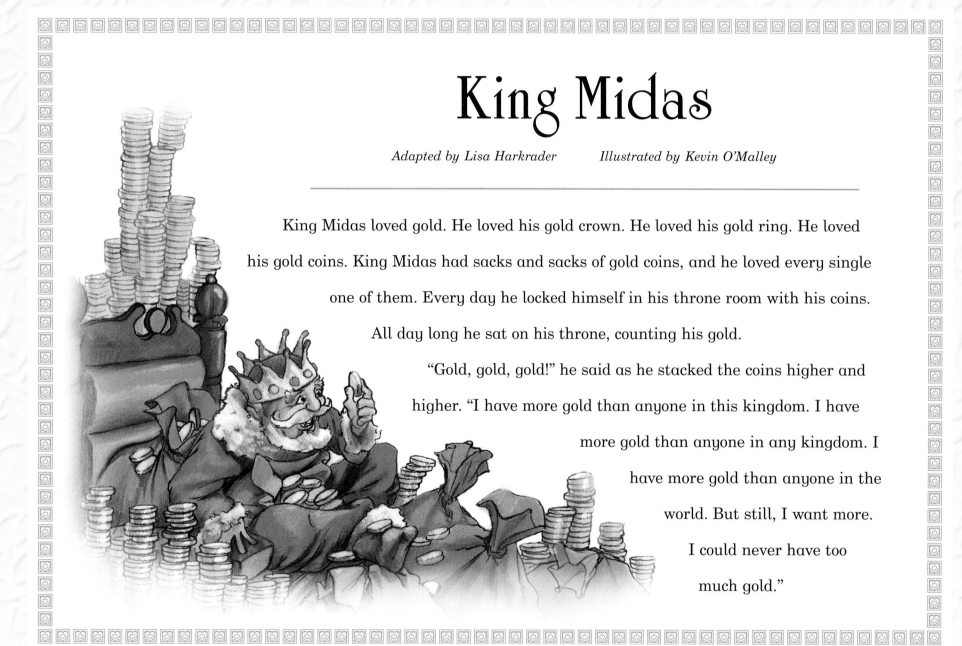

King Midas loved gold. He loved his gold crown. He loved his gold ring. He loved his gold coins. King Midas had sacks and sacks of gold coins, and he loved every single one of them. Every day he locked himself in his throne room with his coins. All day long he sat on his throne, counting his gold.

"Gold, gold, gold!" he said as he stacked the coins higher and higher. "I have more gold than anyone in this kingdom. I have more gold than anyone in any kingdom. I have more gold than anyone in the world. But still, I want more. I could never have too much gold."

Yes, King Midas loved gold.

But there was one thing he loved more. He loved his daughter, Emma.

Emma did not love gold. She loved her garden.

And Emma loved her roses most of all.

"Roses smell so sweet," she said. "Rose petals feel so soft. Roses are pretty colors."

Emma thought that roses were better than gold.

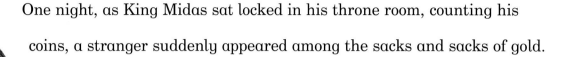

One night, as King Midas sat locked in his throne room, counting his coins, a stranger suddenly appeared among the sacks and sacks of gold.

"Who are you?" asked King Midas.

"My name is not important," said the stranger.

"Where did you come from?" asked King Midas. "The door was locked. How did you get through?"

"I have many talents," said the stranger. "I can do many things." He looked at the piles of coins. "You certainly have a lot of gold. In fact, I'd say you have enough gold for ten kings."

"Enough gold?" laughed King Midas. "No! I could never have enough!"

"If you really believe that you could never have enough gold," said the stranger, "I could make it so. I could make it so that you would always have more gold. I could make it so that everything you touch would turn to gold. Is that what you want?"

"Yes!" said King Midas without hesitation.

The stranger smiled. "Very well. Starting tomorrow morning, everything you touch will turn to gold."

King Midas went straight to bed. He stayed there till morning.

"It is morning!" said King Midas.

He touched his blanket. The blanket turned to gold. He touched his slippers. The slippers turned to gold, too.

"It worked!" he said. "I must tell Emma."

King Midas ran to the garden. He picked a rose. The rose turned to gold.

King Midas ran from bush to bush, touching each rose. Each rose turned to gold under his fingertips. "Emma will be so pleased," he said. "I'll turn all her roses into gold. Now they'll never wilt, and they'll never die. They'll always stay exactly the way they are now: shiny and golden and perfect. She'll love them more than she ever loved them before."

Soon every last rose had been turned into gold. "Won't Emma be surprised?" said King Midas. "I'll touch everything in the garden. Everything will be shiny and golden and perfect. Emma will have the most beautiful garden in the world."

King Midas ran along the garden path. The stones turned to gold beneath his feet. He opened the garden gate. It turned to gold under his hand. He brushed his arm against the garden wall. The wall, too, instantly turned to gold.

"Gold! Gold! Gold! Everything I touch is gold!" cried King Midas. "This is better than anything I could have ever imagined."

Soon King Midas was hungry. He went into the castle to eat breakfast.

The king sat down. His chair turned to gold.

He picked up his fork. The fork turned to gold.

He picked up a grape with his fork. He put the grape in his mouth. He tried to chew.

"Ouch!" cried the king.
"I almost broke my tooth."

The grape
had turned
to gold, too.

King Midas tried to eat a piece of toast, but it turned to gold in his hand. He tried to take a sip of milk, but it turned to gold as soon as it touched his lips. King Midas stared at the golden food. "If everything I touch turns to gold," he said, "how will I ever eat? I'll starve!" But King Midas didn't have time to worry about his food. The door banged open and Emma burst into the room.

"Father!" she cried. "Father, something awful has happened. All my lovely roses are hard and yellow and shiny. They don't smell sweet. The petals aren't soft. They don't fill the garden with lovely colors. They're ruined."

"Ruined?" said King Midas. "What nonsense! Your roses aren't ruined. They're better than ever. They're gold."

"Gold?" said Emma. "But I don't want gold. I want roses. *Real* roses! Sweet and soft, bright red and pink. Please, Father. Do something."

"I will," said King Midas. "I'll get you more roses. They'll be sweet and soft and colorful. I promise. Please stop crying, Emma." He patted his daughter's arm. Instantly she turned to gold.

King Midas began to cry.

His tears turned to gold.

"I have more gold than ever," he said. "But I have lost Emma. I want her back!"

All of a sudden, the stranger was there.

"Please tell me how to get Emma back!" said King Midas.

"Go to the river beside the rose garden," said the stranger.

"When you get to the river," continued the stranger, "dive in and let the water run over you. It will wash away your power to turn things to gold."

"But what about Emma?" asked the king. "How will I turn her back into my dear daughter?"

"Bring back enough water to splash onto the things you turned to gold," said the stranger. "Everything will instantly turn back into what it was before."

King Midas leaped to his feet. He raced around the castle gathering buckets and pitchers. He carried them all down to the river and dove in. He let the water wash over him. The river turned into gold all around him, and then the gold water washed downstream until the water ran clear again.

King Midas filled the buckets and pitchers with the clear water and ran back to the castle. His golden Emma was still standing in the dining hall. King Midas poured a pitcher of water over her head. The gold faded.

Emma blinked her eyes. "Oh, Father! Thank you."

King Midas brought more buckets of water into the castle.

He splashed water on the gold grapes. They turned purple and sweet.

He splashed water on his gold blanket. It turned soft and warm.

He ran into the garden. He splashed water on the roses.
They turned red and pink.

"Are you going to keep any of the gold?"
asked Emma.

"No," said King Midas.
"I do not need gold. I have
something more important.
I have you."

Cinderella

Adapted by Brooke Zimmerman

Illustrated by Sarah Kranz

Cinderella was a lovely girl who lived a long time ago.

She was always cheerful and never grumpy, not even when life was hard.

And life was often hard for Cinderella. You see, she lived with her stepmother

and two stepsisters, who treated Cinderella horribly. The stepmother and

stepsisters felt ugly compared to the beautiful Cinderella, and their jealousy

made them bitter and mean. They did not understand that Cinderella's beauty

came from within her heart. If they could have learned to be kind and loving,

maybe the stepmother and stepsisters would have been beautiful, too.

Instead, they were cruel to Cinderella day in and day out. The

stepmother and stepsisters made Cinderella do all the chores.

The stepmother and stepsisters were very bossy.

"Cinderella, do the dishes!" they said.

"Cinderella, wash the windows!" they said.

"Cinderella, scrub the steps!" they said.

"Cinderella, shine my shoes!" they said.

"Cinderella, bake some bread!" they said.

Cinderella worked hard all day. At night, Cinderella was very tired. Every day was the same. Poor Cinderella.

One morning as Cinderella was ironing the stepsisters' ruffled petticoats, a royal messenger arrived with an invitation. The Prince was having a ball that very evening, and all the ladies in the kingdom were invited!

The stepmother and stepsisters were so excited that they jumped up and down. Then they realized that there was a lot of work to do to get ready—that is, a lot of work for Cinderella to do.

Immediately the stepsisters began making demands of Cinderella. Their dresses had to be trimmed with lace and pearls. Their jewelry had to be polished to a high shine. Their hair had to be styled just so. Cinderella toiled for hours. As she worked, a thought came to her mind.

"Stepmother," she said, "may I go to the ball, too?"

"Ha! Of course not!" replied the stepmother. "You have yet to do all your chores! And just think, such a dirty girl at the ball… ridiculous!"

Of course Cinderella had not yet had time to do her chores or to tidy herself up, since she had been helping the stepsisters all day. But the stepmother did not care. Cinderella was not allowed to go.

The stepmother and stepsisters left for the ball. Cinderella was so sad.

She went out to the garden. She began to cry. "I wish I could go to the ball," said Cinderella.

Then a fairy flew down from the sky! It was Cinderella's fairy godmother.

"Do you want go to the ball, Cinderella?" asked the fairy.

"Oh yes!" said Cinderella. "I do want to go to the ball!"

"I can make your wish come true," said the fairy godmother.

"Oh, that would be wonderful!" Cinderella gasped. "If I could go to the ball, I would be the happiest girl alive!" Then Cinderella thought a moment. "But how will I get to the castle?" she asked.

Since Cinderella's godmother was a fairy, she could make special things happen. "Bring me a pumpkin, and six mice, and a nice fat rat, please, dear," she said to Cinderella.

Cinderella did as she was told. With a tap of her wand, the fairy godmother turned the pumpkin into a coach, the mice into lovely gray horses, and the rat into a handsome coachman! Cinderella was delighted.

There was just one thing left to do. With a graceful flick of her wrist, the fairy godmother tapped Cinderella with her wand. Instantly, Cinderella's ragged clothing became a beautiful gown woven of pure golden thread. As Cinderella marveled at the gown, she felt a tingling on her feet. She looked down and saw glimmering, shimmering slippers made of glass. The fairy shoes perfectly fit Cinderella's dainty feet, and felt as light as air.

"Just remember this, Cinderella," said the fairy godmother. "At the stroke of twelve, the spell will be broken. Everything will return to what it was before—the dress, the coach, everything! You must leave the ball before midnight!"

"I will not be late! Thank you so much, fairy godmother," said Cinderella.

Cinderella stepped into the coach. The fairy godmother waved good-bye. The coach drove away.

Soon they were at the castle. Cinderella stepped out of the coach. She waved good-bye to the coachman.

"See you at midnight!" said Cinderella.

When Cinderella walked into the castle's grand ballroom, a hush fell over the crowd. Everyone turned to stare at the graceful maiden who had appeared in the doorway. Soon the people began to whisper.

"Who is she? Is she a princess?" they murmured. No one knew. "How lovely she is!" someone said. Everyone nodded in agreement.

Hearing all the hubbub, the prince turned to see the cause of the excitement. He looked at Cinderella, and their eyes met across the room. And just that quickly, Cinderella and the prince fell in love.

Cinderella and the prince danced together all evening. In fact, the prince would dance with no one else. As they glided across the floor, Cinderella and the prince spoke softly to one another. No one could quite hear what they were saying, but they both looked completely enchanted with one another.

Cinderella was so happy at the ball that she forgot all about her fairy godmother's warning.

Then a clock began to chime. The clock chimed one … two … three.

"The prince is a good dancer!" thought Cinderella.
The clock chimed four … five … six.

"I am having such a good time!" thought Cinderella.
The clock chimed seven … eight … nine.

"What did my fairy godmother tell me?" wondered
Cinderella. The clock chimed ten … eleven ….

"Oh no!" thought Cinderella. The spell would end at midnight!
She ran away as fast as she could. She ran so fast that one of
her slippers slipped off. She had to leave it behind.

Then the clock chimed twelve!

Cinderella dashed out of the ballroom quick as a flash. The prince was quite shocked. He noticed the glass slipper she had left behind, picked it up, and placed it carefully in the pocket of his coat.

For a few days thereafter, the prince could think of nothing but his lovely dance partner. Determined to find her, he sent out a royal decree that every maiden in the kingdom must try on the slipper. The prince would visit every home himself to make sure no one was missed.

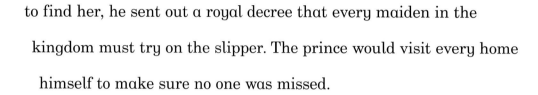

Finally the day came when the prince knocked on the door of Cinderella's house. Of course the stepsisters tried on the slipper first. They tugged and pulled and pushed, but the slipper was just too small. Then it was Cinderella's turn.

"Bah!" scoffed the stepmother. "Don't waste your time on Cinderella. The slipper won't fit her dirty foot!"

But the prince didn't hear what the stepmother said. He was already looking deep into Cinderella's eyes. He held his breath and slid the slipper onto her foot.

"It fits!" said the prince.

"It fits?" yelled the stepmother and stepsisters.

"Yes," said Cinderella. "It fits."

Soon after that day, the prince and Cinderella were married. Cinderella was now a princess! The prince and Cinderella were very happy. They loved each other very much.

The stepmother and stepsisters were sorry for being mean to Cinderella. Cinderella said she loved them anyway. She said they could live in the castle, too.

At last the stepmother and stepsisters saw that Cinderella was more than just a pretty face. She was beautiful because she was kind.

The Frog Prince

Adapted by Rebecca Grazulis   Illustrated by Judy Love

One beautiful summer afternoon, a pretty young princess decided to take a walk by herself in a wood. Humming happily, she set out among the trees. Her faithful cat followed her, and she was glad for the company.

The princess and the cat strolled through the woods until they came to a sparkling spring of water. The princess skipped to the water's edge and dipped her hand into the spring.

"How cool the water is!" she exclaimed, delighted.

In her other hand, the princess held a shiny golden ball. She loved to play with it. In fact, it was her very favorite thing. She was always throwing it up into the air and catching it again as it fell.

"Whee!" she would yell as she tossed the ball as high as she could.

The princess threw the ball. It went up … and up … and up. It was so far away that she could not see it.

Then the ball fell. It fell very fast.

The princess did not catch the ball this time.

Splash! The ball fell into the spring.
The princess looked into the spring.
It was very deep.

And the golden ball was at the bottom.

The princess started to cry. "I want my ball back!" she said.

The princess wept bitterly. Her heart was very heavy. "I would give away all my fancy clothes and expensive jewels," she exclaimed, "just to have my ball again." The princess sniffled and fought back a few tears. "In fact," she continued, "I would give everything I have in the world!"

As the princess spoke, a frog clambered out of the water onto a lily pad. He wanted to see the face that belonged to such a sad voice.

"Princess," said the frog, "why do you weep so?"

"Who are you to speak to me, you nasty frog?" asked the princess cruelly. "You can do nothing for me! My favorite golden ball has fallen into this spring. I fear it is lost forever!"

"I want not your jewels and fine clothes," the frog said gently, with a cloud of sadness in his eyes. "But if you will love me, and let me eat from your plate, I will bring you your ball again."

The princess did not know what to do.

She thought about her ball. She wanted it back. But she did not want a slimy frog to eat with her!

"Can you really get my ball?" the princess asked the frog.

The frog nodded.

"Okay," she said, "then I will grant your wish!"

But the princess was not telling the truth.

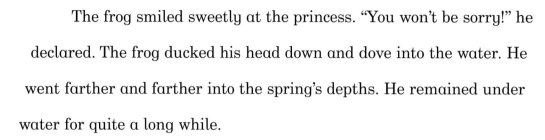

The frog smiled sweetly at the princess. "You won't be sorry!" he declared. The frog ducked his head down and dove into the water. He went farther and farther into the spring's depths. He remained under water for quite a long while.

"Where is that slimy frog?" the princess wondered with irritation.

Just when the princess was sure she would never see the frog again, his green head popped out of the water. High above his head, he held the golden ball! He threw it onto the spring's shore triumphantly.

The princess ran to pick up the ball and hugged it tight to her chest.

"Oh, my beautiful, perfect golden ball!" she said. "I will never lose you again!" Then the princess began to skip home. She was so overjoyed that she never even thought to thank the frog.

"Wait, princess!" called the frog. "Take me with you as you promised!"

But as she skipped away into the distance, the princess didn't hear a word the frog said. She was too busy being careful with the golden ball.

The next day the princess was eating supper. She heard a noise.

Something was coming up the stairs. The princess heard a knock at the door.

"Come out, princess dear!" said a little voice. "Your true love is here!"

The princess ran to the door. It was the frog who had helped her!

"Ack!" yelled the princess.

The princess was scared. She shut the door. She ran back to the table.

The king could see that something had frightened his daughter. "Daughter," he said, "whatever is the matter?" The princess explained to her father what had happened. Meanwhile, the frog continued to knock.

The king looked sternly at his daughter. "You made a promise," he said, "and you must keep it. Let him in." The princess dragged herself to the castle's entrance and opened the door. The frog hopped right in.

"Lift me up onto the table, princess dear," said the frog, "so I can sit beside you." The princess obeyed. Then the frog made another request.

"Put your plate near me, princess dear," he said, "so I can eat off it."

"Sheesh!" exclaimed the princess. "So demanding!" But the princess did as the frog asked, and the frog ate as much as he could. After dinner, the frog wiped his mouth with the princess's napkin and hopped away.

"Gone at last!" said the princess. But the frog came back the next night.

The frog ate dinner with the princess again. After he ate, the frog left.

"Finally!" yelled the princess. But the next night the frog came back a third time.

The frog ate dinner with the princess again. Then he hopped off the table.

When the princess and the king looked down on the floor, the frog was gone.

There was a prince instead!

The princess could not believe her eyes! He was the most handsome prince she had ever seen. And he was sprawled out on the floor, gazing at her adoringly. "Where did you come from?" she asked.

"Don't you recognize me?" the prince said with a grin.

The princess stared at him for a moment. "No," she replied honestly.

"I believe I rescued your favorite golden ball," said the prince. The princess looked very confused. "Let me explain," began the prince. "I was enchanted by a cruel fairy, who changed me into a frog. I had to remain a frog until a princess allowed me to eat from her plate for three nights."

"Oh my!" exclaimed the princess. She was more than a little surprised. "And I…I was so mean to you. Can you ever forgive me?"

"You are forgiven, princess dear," said the prince, "for you have broken the spell. Now my only wish is to marry you and love you as long as we live."

Now, the princess knew a good thing when she saw it. The prince and princess were married the very next day.

The wedding day was a very happy one.

A carriage drove up. It was pulled by four beautiful gray horses.

"We will live happily ever after!" said the princess.

The princess kissed her father and said good-bye.

The prince and princess rode away in the carriage.

And the princess was right. They did live happily ever after.

Sleeping Beauty

Adapted by Lora Kalkman   *Illustrated by Holly Jones*

A long time ago there lived a king and queen with joyous news.

After years of praying, they had been blessed with a baby. They named

their daughter Lillyanna. They decided to celebrate the princess's

birth by throwing a lavish banquet for everyone in the kingdom.

While they were busy preparing invitations, the queen looked

up with a frown. "What about Griselda, the wicked fairy?"

she asked. "She will surely be angry if she is not invited."

"Griselda is nasty and mean," the king declared.

"She is not welcome at our celebration."

"Very well," said the queen, although she was more

than a little worried.

At the party, everyone brought gifts to the princess. Three good fairies brought gifts, too.

The first fairy gave the gift of beauty. The second fairy gave the gift of wisdom.

Just then, Griselda stormed in! She was angry. "How dare you not invite me?" she asked. "I have a gift for the princess, too."

But Griselda's gift was a wicked spell.

"The princess will prick her finger on the spindle of a spinning wheel," she said. "She will die before she is fully grown." Griselda laughed an evil laugh and ran out of the castle.

Luckily, the tiniest good fairy still had a gift to give. She went to the baby and whispered, "My gift to you is true love. While I cannot undo Griselda's spell, I can alter it a bit. Instead of dying when you prick your finger, you will merely fall asleep. You shall be awakened by the kiss of your true love."

The years passed, and Lillyanna grew into a beautiful young girl. One evening, as Lillyanna walked through the castle alone, she noticed a hallway she'd never seen before. It led to a small room where a woman was spinning wool at a spinning wheel. Lillyanna did not recognize Griselda in disguise.

"Come closer, dearie," Griselda beckoned. "Look at this beautiful thread." As Lillyanna drew near, Griselda grabbed her hand. She pricked the girl's finger on the spindle.

"Ouch!" cried Princess Lillyanna. She fell to the floor in a deep, deep sleep.

The king and queen found the sleeping princess.

They could not wake her up.

They called the doctor. But the doctor could not wake her up.

They called a wizard. But the wizard could not wake her up.

They called the good fairies. Even the fairies could not wake her up.

But the tiniest fairy knew what to do. She waved her magic wand. She made everyone else in the castle fall asleep, too.

The fairies laid the princess to sleep in her royal bed. "Don't worry," the tiniest fairy whispered in Princess Lillyanna's ear. "We will find a prince to rescue you."

The fairies flitted about the land in search of a prince. First, they came upon Prince Leopold. "He seems suitable," thought the fairies. So while the prince was asleep, they used their magic to send him a dream about the sleeping beauty.

"I must find the girl of my dreams," announced Prince Leopold when he awoke. He set out for the castle, with the fairies guiding his path. But alas, the castle was overgrown with thorny bushes and prickly trees. As the prince tried to cut his way through to the castle door, he, too, fell asleep.

"This is the work of Griselda," one fairy declared angrily. "We cannot undo her wicked spells."

"That is true," replied the tiniest fairy. "Instead, we must find the prince that is Lillyanna's true love. Love shall always prevail over Griselda's evil."

The fairies set out to find Princess Lillyanna's true love.

They made Prince Hugo dream about the sleeping beauty. He went to find her. But when he came to the castle, he fell asleep.

They made Prince Monty dream about the sleeping beauty. He went to find her. But when he came to the castle, he fell asleep, too.

The fairies were upset. Who would be Princess Lillyanna's true love?

The tiniest fairy searched the land. She finally came upon a promising prince named Darius. "He is both good and wise. He could be the one," she thought excitedly.

That night, while Prince Darius was sleeping, the tiniest fairy worked her magic. She sent him a dream about Princess Lillyanna. The next day, she hid nearby while the prince enjoyed breakfast with his father.

"I had an incredible dream last night," Prince Darius said, and he told his father about his vision of the sleeping beauty. The surprised king told his son the true story of Princess Lillyanna. After hearing the tale, the fearless and determined Prince Darius set out for Lillyanna's castle. When he reached the thicket of thorny bushes and prickly trees, he drew his sword and sliced through the bramble with ease. The good fairies, who were hiding nearby, cheered happily.

Prince Darius cut the prickly branches. He cut the thorny bushes.

"This is easy!" he said.

Prince Darius cut and cut. He did not fall asleep. Finally, he got to the castle door.

Prince Darius went inside. He searched for the girl in his dreams.

At last he found Princess Lillyanna. "She is beautiful," Prince Darius said.

Then he kissed her hand.

Instantly, Griselda's evil spell was broken! Lillyanna's eyes fluttered open. She smiled at the handsome prince standing beside her. Prince Darius told Lillyanna everything that had occurred. Meanwhile, everyone else in the castle awoke, too. Thanks to the good fairies' magic, they did not know what had happened. The king and queen rushed to check on their daughter. They were elated to see her awake, and as radiant as ever.

"Who are you?" the king asked when he saw Prince Darius. The prince told the king about his dream and his mission. "When I kissed Princess Lillyanna, she awoke," he explained.

"How can we ever thank you?" the king asked Prince Darius. "You may have anything in the kingdom."

"There is only one thing I request," said the prince. "May I have your daughter's hand in marriage?"

"Yes!" said the king, the queen, and Lillyanna.

The tiniest fairy was hiding nearby. She was very happy.
She had found Princess Lillyanna's true love.

Soon it was time for the wedding.
Everyone brought gifts.

The tiniest fairy gave
the very last gift.

"You will live
happily ever after,"
said the fairy.

And they did.

Rumpelstiltskin

Adapted by Kurt Hettinger

Illustrated by Burgandy Nilles

Once upon a time there lived a tailor who was overly boastful. One morning he was carrying on an argument with a baker in the marketplace. The baker had bragged that his daughter could bake moldy flour into golden bread.

The tailor replied, much too loudly, "That is nothing! My daughter can spin moldy straw into golden thread!"

As it happened, the king was passing just at that moment and overheard the tailor. The king said to him, "If your daughter is as skillful as you say, bring her this night to my palace, and she will be put to the test. But if she is unable to do as you say, then both you and she shall die."

So later that day, the tailor took his daughter to the palace.
The king took her to a room full of straw.

The king was mean. He said,
"Spin this straw into gold."
Then he locked the door.

But no one can spin straw
into gold. The girl felt afraid.
She began to cry.

Just then the door opened.
A little man walked in.

He said, "Why are you sad?
Is it really that bad?"

"I'm crying," answered the girl, "because I must spin this straw into gold or be killed. But I can't do it."

She was so upset, she did not even wonder who the strange man was or how he had entered the locked room.

The little man rubbed his chin. "Hmmm. Spin straw into gold so you may live. If I do this thing, what might you give?"

"I can give you my necklace," said the girl, pulling the necklace over her head.

The little man took the necklace and placed it around his neck. He then seated himself on the stool in front of the spinning wheel, turned it three times, and the spool was filled with golden thread! Then he put another empty spool on, and soon it was filled as well. He worked all night, until many spools were filled with golden thread. He left when he was done.

At dawn the king arrived with his guards. When he saw the gold he was surprised and delighted, but his heart became greedy. He took the tailor's daughter into a larger room filled with straw. "Spin all of this straw into gold before tomorrow," he commanded, "if you value your life."

Then he locked the door. The tailor's daughter cried all day long.

That night, the little man came back. He said, "I will do the task. Another gift is all I ask."

"You can have my ring," said the girl.

The little man began to work. Soon he had turned all the straw into gold.

The greedy king was happy when he saw the gold.

He took the girl into another room full of straw. He said, "If you spin this third room of straw into gold, you will be my queen."

When the girl was alone, the strange little man visited her a third time. He looked around the room and said, "All of this straw still to be spun … what would you give for this to be done?"

"I have already given you the only things I had," answered the girl. "I have nothing left to give."

The little man said, "Then promise that when you become queen, you'll give your firstborn child to me."

The girl didn't like the dark look in the little man's eyes. "But if I do not agree," she thought to herself, "I will never become queen at all." She didn't know what else to do, so she said, "I promise."

The little man set to spinning the straw into gold. When the king arrived again at dawn, he found all the straw spun as he had commanded. The king married the girl that very day, and so the tailor's young daughter became a queen.

A year later, the queen had a baby.

She forgot all about the little man.
She forgot about her promise, too.

But one night, the little man
came back. He wanted to take
the baby away.

The queen was so sad!
She began to cry.

But the little man was having
fun. It was all a game to him. He said,
"I will give you three days to guess my
name. If you can do it, you win the game."

That night the queen stayed up all night making a list of every name she had ever heard. She also sent a trusted messenger into the countryside to inquire far and wide for any other possible names.

When the little man returned the next day, the queen began to read all the names on her list. She asked, "Is your name Adam, Allen, Anwar, or Arnold?

"Please, please! It's none of these," replied the little man. The queen went on, reading names such as Bartholomew and Andrew, Donald and Ronald, Frederick and George. But after the queen read each name, the little man would sing, "Nor is that my name! Oh, I do enjoy this game!" Soon the queen had read her entire list, but she still had not discovered the correct name. The little man left, and the queen set to work making another list of names—the stranger, the better.

The next day, the little man came back. The queen read her new list. But all those names were wrong, too.

That night, the queen's messenger came back.

He said, "I have found one new name. I was in the woods. I saw a fire. There was a little man who danced around the fire. And he sang this song:

'Here I come, there I go,
This is my favorite game.
The queen will never know
Rum–pel–stilt–skin is my name!'"

The queen was filled with happiness when she heard this new strange name. She knew in her heart that Rumpelstiltskin must be the little man's name. That night she slept well.

The next day when the little man arrived, he said, "Today is the day we end our game. Now, missus queen, what is my name?" The queen was smiling, confident that she would soon be free of her awful promise to the strange little man. The man looked at her with great curiosity. "Make a guess," he prodded, "or give me the child. And I'll take the baby back to the wild."

And so the queen began to name names for the last time. "Is your name Bill? Or Will?" she asked innocently. "Fie and blame! Those names have been named!" the man scolded. "And now I tire of this game!" The little man started to grab the baby away from the queen.

"Just one more guess," said the queen.
"Is your name ... Rum–pel–stilt–skin?"

"Drat! Scat! Who told you that?!"
yelled the man named Rumpelstiltskin.

He was **very** angry. He shook his
fist in the air. Then he stomped out
of the castle.

He never came back. No one ever
saw Rumpelstiltskin again.

And so the queen was free of her
promise. She and her child lived
happily ever after.

Thumbelina

Adapted by Leslie Lindecker   Illustrated by Jane Maday

Once a woman lived alone in a lovely little house. She tended her garden carefully and had raised beautiful flowers all around. One sunny day she met a wise woman passing her gate. The wise woman stopped to admire the garden.

"If only I had a child to share the garden's beauty with," the woman wished out loud. "Then I would be truly happy."

The wise woman smiled. "Take this seed," she said. "Plant it in your garden, and tend it with love. You will see what will happen."

"Thank you!" said the woman.

She planted the seed in her garden. It was in a sunny spot. She watered the seed, too.

Soon a flower began to grow.

A pretty bud sprang up from the leaves.

One day, the petals popped open!

Inside the flower there was a tiny girl. She was as little as a thumb!

"I shall call you 'Thumbelina,' because you are no bigger than my thumb," the woman told the girl. The tiny girl giggled, and it sounded like fairies were ringing bells.

Thumbelina and the woman lived happily together for a long time. Thumbelina was so happy she sang all day long. Unfortunately, her singing attracted a large, ugly, wet toad from the stream by the garden. One night the toad hopped in through an open window. She stared at Thumbelina.

"This lovely creature would make a fine wife for my son," the toad croaked. She gently picked up Thumbelina and hopped out the window.

The toad put Thumbelina on a lily pad in the middle of the stream and went to get her son. But Thumbelina woke up before the toads returned. She was frightened and began to cry.

The fish in the stream felt sad for pretty Thumbelina.

The fish chewed on the stem of
the lily pad so Thumbelina could
float away.

Thumbelina floated down the stream.
She was glad to be away from the toad.

Soon she came to a green field.

She made a bed out of woven grass.

Thumbelina sang to the birds.

She danced with the butterflies.

She stayed there all summer long.

Too soon the summer sun gave way to autumn breezes. Thumbelina shivered with cold. She knew she had to find some kind of shelter. Tiny Thumbelina walked through the nearby field looking for someplace warm.

All at once she saw a door in front of her. Thumbelina knocked. A tiny field mouse opened the door. She squinted at Thumbelina through tiny glasses. "Oh, my!" she squeaked. "Come in from the cold, my dear!" The old field mouse was so pleased to have company, she invited Thumbelina to stay while the cold weather lasted.

One day Thumbelina and the old field mouse heard a pecking at the door. Thumbelina opened the door to find a swallow with an injured wing. He could not fly to warmer lands like the other birds, and he was growing very cold. Thumbelina invited him inside.

"Fetch warm blankets to wrap him in," said the field mouse. "I will bring berries and broth to feed him."

All winter long, Thumbelina and
the mouse took care of the bird.

They sat by the fire.

They sang songs.

They stayed warm and snug
in the little mouse house.

Thumbelina, the mouse,
and the bird all became
very good friends.

And soon the bird's wing
grew strong again.

Winter passed quickly for the three friends. Soon the spring thaw was followed by new leaves on the trees and flowers popping their colorful heads up out of the ground.

Each day the swallow tested his wing, flying farther and farther from the old field mouse's den. He came back later each day. One day the swallow did not come back. Thumbelina was sad. "We knew he would go home some day," she said to her friend the field mouse. "But I will miss him."

"So will I," sighed the field mouse. "But he must be glad to get home."

A week later Thumbelina was outside the field mouse's den when she heard, "Tweet! Tweet-tweet!" Thumbelina looked up and saw her friend the swallow. He flew above her head, then landed in the field beside her.

"You must come home with me!" he sang.

Thumbelina looked surprised. "You told us about your home. It's very far away. I cannot walk that far."

The mouse came outside to see what was going on.

The mouse was very happy to see the bird.

Thumbelina told the mouse what the bird said.

"That sounds like fun!" the field mouse said. "You should go."

"But how can I get there? I cannot fly," Thumbelina said.

The swallow had the answer. "You are light as a feather," he said. "You can ride on my back as I fly home."

Thumbelina hugged the old field mouse. "I will miss you," she said.

The field mouse dabbed her eyes with a bit of cloth. "Be sure to remember all your adventures so you can tell me when you come back for a visit," she said.

Thumbelina climbed onto the swallow's back. The bird rose up in the air, high above the field. High above the field mouse's den. High above the forest, then high over the highest mountains. They came to a blue lake shaded by tall trees and lovely flowers.

"This is my home," the bird said. "Now it will be your home." He gently set Thumbelina down on a large white flower. She looked around.

In the center of each flower was a tiny man or woman. They were the same size as Thumbelina! She had never seen anyone as small as she was. They each had delicate wings on their shoulders and could flit from flower to flower. They smiled and waved at her.

Thumbelina turned when she heard someone say her name.

A tiny man stood in the center of a flower. He wore a tiny crown on his head. He was a prince.

"How handsome you are," said Thumbelina to the prince.

"How pretty you are," said the prince. "Will you be my queen?" he asked.

"Yes," Thumbelina said.

Then Thumbelina's friend the bird sang his sweetest wedding song for the prince and Thumbelina.

Beauty and the Beast

Adapted by Rebecca Grazulis   *Illustrated by David Merrell*

Once upon a time there was a very wealthy man who lived a happy and prosperous life with his family. The man had three sons, all of whom were strong, and three daughters, all of whom were beautiful. The youngest daughter was especially beautiful, even more so than the others. From the time she was a very little girl, everyone would always tell her how pretty she was. "How handsome your eyes are!" someone would say. "And your hair is so dark and lovely!" someone else would chime in. Everyone admired her. Her father even called her "the little beauty." And years later, when she had grown to be a beautiful young woman, she still went by the name of Beauty.

But Beauty's father lost his money. The family became poor.

Beauty's father decided to go to the city. He hoped he could make more money there.

"What do you want me to bring back, Beauty?" asked her father.

"Just a rose," said Beauty.

Beauty's father went to the city. But he did not find any work. So he left the city. On the way home, Beauty's father got lost … and found a castle!

Beauty's father guided his horse into the stable and entered the castle. He found himself in a gigantic hall with a roaring fire. He warmed himself before the fire's glow. He noticed that the table was set and piled high with delicious-looking food. "What a feast!" cried Beauty's father. He waited for his host to arrive. He waited, and he waited, and he waited. Finally, he could wait no longer. "I'm sure my host will understand," he said as he took a bite. After he ate, Beauty's father wandered through the castle. He saw many magnificent things, but he stopped when he entered a bedroom. Since it was so late, he decided to go to sleep.

In the morning, Beauty's father found a suit of clothes lying beside the bed. "A kind fairy must live here!" he thought happily. He put on the clothes and went to find his horse. On his way to the stable, he passed through a rose garden.

"My Beauty wanted a rose," he remembered suddenly. He reached down to the rose bushes and plucked a single red rose.

Then Beauty's father heard a loud noise. It was a beast! "Why did you pick my rose?" asked the angry beast. "I was kind to you!"

"I am sorry," said Beauty's father. "The rose is for my daughter."

"I will forgive you," said the beast, "if you send your daughter to live with me."

Beauty's father went back to his family. He gave the rose to Beauty. Then he told her about the beast.

"I must go back," he said.

"No, Father," said Beauty. "I will go."

Beauty arrived at the castle and found her dinner ready in the great hall. Just as she was about to sit down, the beast entered the hall.

"May I join you?" asked the beast.

"As you please," answered Beauty bravely. By the time Beauty finished eating her dinner, she had nearly conquered her fear of the beast. She learned that he was actually quite kind. Then the beast said something that almost made Beauty faint.

"Beauty," said the beast, "will you be my wife?"

Beauty did not know what to say. She was afraid of making the beast angry. Finally she said, "No, Beast."

The beast gave a sigh that echoed through the whole castle. "Then farewell, Beauty," he said sadly, and left the room. But for nearly three months after that day, the beast visited Beauty every evening during supper. Beauty eventually grew quite fond of him, and soon they became great friends.

One day Beauty said, "Please let me go see my father, Beast."

"You may go see your father," said the beast, "but you must come back. I will die without you."

"Do not worry," said Beauty. "I will be back in a week."

The beast gave Beauty a trunk. It was full of gifts for Beauty's family. There was gold, and diamonds, and fine clothes.

Beauty went home. She hugged her father. He was very happy to see his daughter.

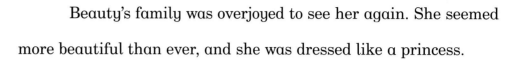

Beauty's family was overjoyed to see her again. She seemed more beautiful than ever, and she was dressed like a princess.

Time flew too quickly for the happily reunited family, and soon an entire week had passed. Beauty announced that she had to return to the beast's castle. Beauty's beloved sisters were so saddened by the thought of Beauty leaving them again that Beauty promised to stay one week more.

But Beauty could not help thinking about the beast, whom she had grown to love dearly. The tenth night that she was at her father's house, Beauty dreamed that the beast was lying in the palace garden, dying. She awoke with a start.

"I am so unkind!" cried Beauty. "The beast has tried to please me in every way. It isn't his fault he is so ugly. The important thing is that he is kind and good. I should have agreed to be his wife."

Beauty went back to the castle. She could not find the beast. She was worried.

"Where could he be?" she wondered.

Beauty found the beast in the garden. He was sick. Beauty sat down next to him.

"You were gone too long," said the beast. "I missed you too much. I cannot live."

"No, Beast," said Beauty. "Do not die. Live to marry me."

As soon as Beauty said these words, the castle began to sparkle with light. Beauty looked back to her dear beast. But to her great surprise, the beast had turned into the most handsome prince that Beauty had ever seen. He quickly thanked her for putting an end to the charm that had kept him a beast for so long.

"But I don't understand," said Beauty. "Where is my beloved beast?"

The prince smiled. "You see him before you," he replied. "A wicked fairy turned me into a beast, and I had to remain a beast until someone with an open heart would agree to marry me. You, Beauty, are the only one who was generous enough with her love to break the spell. Today I offer you my crown."

Beauty was very surprised, but happily so. She gave the charming prince her hand, and together they entered the castle. Beauty was thrilled to find her whole family in the great hall. She thought that this must be the best moment of her life.

Beauty married the prince on a beautiful spring day.

"Your life will be happy," said Beauty's father.

Beauty and the prince smiled at each other. They knew they would be happy.

"I would do anything for you," said the prince to his bride.

Beauty went with the prince to his kingdom. His people were glad he was back. And they loved their new Princess Beauty.

The two lived there many years. Their castle was always a happy place.

The End